" Someone has been sleeping in my bed.
And she's still here, Mama." - Baby Bear

To My Mama Bear
& Baby Bear

ISBN: 978-0-9968453-0-4

Story, Design, and Illustration by P. Tanasit.

GOLDILOCKS

And The Three Bears.

P. Tanasit

 a RedwagonMouse Book

It was a year ago when they saw a little girl run out of their house.

"Who was she?" The Bears asked themselves. "And why was she here? What did she want?"

No one really knew for certain.

But surely it was someone, or something, that sat in their chairs. Slept in their beds. Ate their porridge. And all at once vanished, never to be seen again.

The more they pondered on the event, the more restless they became, and so it was decided that they would never speak of the presence again.

Mama Bear

Baby Bear

Papa Bear

BEAR FAMILY

That was a year ago.

It was exactly 3:28 AM when an eerie chill woke Papa Bear up. This was the third time he woke up at this exact time, and always he had the same dream of being lost, wandering in a muddy garden.

"Strange indeed..." Papa Bear muttered to himself. "Why the garden?"

Unable to settle back to sleep, he decided to go downstairs for a glass of water. Yet before he could reach the kitchen, something oddly familiar made Papa Bear suddenly stop.

It was that dream chill again, which he could now feel brushing past his neck.

He glanced around, looking for an explanation.

But there wasn't any. Everything was still and quiet, except for the curtain swaying by the opened window. Papa Bear sighed at the sight.

"She'll never learn until we're robbed and killed," he muttered while shutting the window. He wondered if Mama Bear would get the message if he started leaving the front door open at night.

"Why were you in the garden?" a voice whispered out of the dark, sending Papa Bear's heart out of his chest.

It was only Baby Bear, blankly staring at an empty chair.

Papa Bear began to feel his heart beating again. His son's sleepwalking habits never ceased to unnerve him.

"And where's your mommy?" Baby Bear continued. "Why are you here?"

On many occasions, Papa Bear was tempted to shake his son out of that haunting, hollow stare. But he knew better. Never startle a sleepwalker awake.

So he began, as always, gently ushering his son back to bed.

Returning to his bedroom, Papa Bear thought about a much needed vacation that the family should take together.

"Perhaps a seaside visit.." he amused himself. "Yes, a fishing trip. That would be absolutely..."

Papa Bear noticed something rather odd on the stairway.

A strange smudge. He peered closer. It was mud. Wet mud! Trails of it up and down the stairs.

"Strange, had Baby Bear gone outside sleepwal...?" But Papa didn't finish his thought. He saw his own feet.

They were caked with mud.

In a panic Papa Bear rushed to the bathroom to scrub and wash his feet. He quickly wiped the stairs clean and shot back in bed. There he remained crouched and unmoved.

"This...this is impossible," he thought. "I have never walked in my sleep before!"

Feeling extremely uneasy, he decided it was best not to talk about this, not until certain facts are confirmed.

Besides, Mama Bear would be terribly upset if she found out mud got tracked inside.

The next morning, Mama Bear raised the issue of someone trampling her garden.

"This is not the first time!" she protested. "Must be some rascals in the neighborhood."

Papa Bear diverted the subject to the window being left opened at night. But Mama Bear assured him that she was mindful of closing it nightly.

Papa Bear did not care to push the matter further. There were more pressing concerns now, the feeling as if he was becoming mentally unstable.

The ensuing days were rather uneventful. No mud. No sleepwalking. No chills.

For this, Papa Bear felt grateful.

Until several evenings later...

Mama Bear bolted up in bed in the middle of the night, drenched with sweat. She could feel her pulse racing. Her breath felt like it was struggling against a weight, as if some presence or something was leaning on her chest.

She immediately got out of bed and opened the window. She could feel the night breeze greet her and soon began to feel relieved.

"What's the matter with me? I hadn't skipped my medication, had I?" Mama Bear wondered. "No, perhaps it might have been the late supper."

Whatever was the cause, Mama Bear knew she shouldn't lose any more sleep. She decided to return to bed.

When she got there, a small pale figure stood up from her bed and looked dead at her.

Mama Bear tried to scream, but was unable to choke out a sound.

And then she woke up in a gasp, realizing it was only a dream.

It was just a dream.

As soon as she was able to catch her breath, she noticed that the window had been opened.

"Good heavens, I must have really opened it mid sleep," she thought. "I'm starting to lose my mind."

She immediately got out of bed to close it. And in that moment, Mama Bear saw movement outside the window.

A girl! In her garden.

Mama Bear froze.

No, it must have been something else, she assured herself.

But it sure looked like a little girl.

Then it happened again.

Mama Bear quickly closed the window, but it wouldn't budge. The latch was resisting her.

Mama Bear looked closer and saw hair.

Long, pale blonde hair.

Strands of it had snagged on the latch, and was keeping it from closing. In fact, they were all over the window sill! Whose hair was this?

Mama Bear did not care anymore. She abandoned her effort and quickly buried herself in bed.

She nudged herself closer to Papa Bear. It was definitely the medication she had forgotten to take, she chided herself.

This had to remain a secret for now, as Papa Bear already thought she was crazy.

The next morning, Mama Bear glanced at the window latch and was relieved that she did not see any hair.

She did notice Papa Bear oddly strolling near the garden, but she didn't know he was anxiously checking for more footprints.

Then they caught glimpse of each other and smiled politely from where they stood. Neither was aware that each was living with a terrifying secret that they desperately wanted to confess.

But they needed to be more certain before causing panic, as they had a history of doing.

The following evening, Baby Bear was struggling to sleep. The restless crickets and branches outside his window were bothering him to no end.

"Please, be quiet," Baby Bear pleaded under his breath. "Just for tonight..."

Then, as if by a spell, everything became dead silent. And not just silent, but also cold and still.

Baby Bear sat up immediately and drew his blanket closer. This was not the kind of quiet he liked.

"Papa?" he blurted out weakly.

There were no answers.

But something soon caught his attention--a peculiar sound.

He couldn't make it out. It sounded like a breathy whisper of sort looming from the corner of his room.

Baby Bear listened closer.

No, it was coming from the hallway. It was not Mama or Papa Bear's whispering. And now it was starting to sound like a whimper, like a little girl sobbing.

Then abruptly it stopped. Baby Bear's tiny heart was now galloping. Someone is in the hallway!

Echoes of tiny footsteps soon followed.

"Mama?" Baby Bear called out, sensing the steps creaking towards his door.

"Mama, is that you?"

The footsteps suddenly scrambled away.

Slowly, with the slingshot in his hand, Baby Bear mustered enough courage to peek outside his door.

There was nothing, just an empty hallway.

He immediately went back to bed and hedged himself with the blanket. But how was he supposed to sleep now?

Yet before his head could settle into the pillow, the noise had returned. This time it was neither whispering nor footsteps.

It was the doorknob. And it was turning.

Baby Bear snapped the blanket over his head and squeezed his eyes shut, as if the very act could keep out the nightmare.

"Please go away. Please go away. Please, please..." he gibbered.

It didn't go away.

He could now hear the door yawn open. But why couldn't he hear footsteps? He didn't want to look.

He couldn't.

And he didn't need to. He could feel the chills rising in his spine, that something was near the foot of his bed.

Baby Bear felt paralyzed. He tried to utter prayers, but started to feel his blanket shifting away from him, as if it was being dragged down by a weight.

Baby Bear held it as long he could, but when a cold presence sank into the pillow next to him, he began to scream.

Mama and Papa Bear rushed in.

"I heard noises in the hallway, and it came here! It came to my bed!" Baby Bear blurted.

"What came in here? What?" Papa Bear asked.

"It came in here. I don't know. It laid down next to..."

In between Baby Bear's stammering, Mama Bear pulled a strand of blonde hair from his pillow and immediately passed out.

The next morning they gathered at the table. Each confessed all the strange occurrences: The window being left opened. The strands of blonde hair in the house. The trampled vegetable garden.

Slowly the Bears began recollecting the strange, haunting events that visited them about a year ago, events involving the porridge, the broken chairs, the tousled beds.

And the girl.

The Bears knew at once that they needed help.

The Inspector, who was a man of wisdom and rare intelligence, was soon invited for tea.

The bears relayed the story as faithfully as they had experienced it.

"Having examined the evidence with logic and reasoning, I assure you that you are dealing with a spectre of a restless kind," said the Inspector. "A spirit or ghost of this class is unresolved of its past, and indeed very much uncertain of its future."

"Do you know what it wants?" Papa Bear asked.

There was a sudden crackling shift in the ceiling. A chair fell to the floor, followed by a slight scuffle in the attic. A long silence ensued. Everyone was now gazing at the ceiling, anticipating the next shift.

"Spirits are bound by laws that operate beyond the realm of physical science," the Inspector continued. "They have a limited field of communication. They will try to communicate in symbols, like the language of dreams."

"You have 3:28 AM, the precise time you were awakened," the Inspector added.

"You have the garden persistently trampled by a sleepwalker!"

"Then the bizarre manifestations of hair!"

"So what does it all mean?" Mama Bear asked.

The Inspector took a long deep pause.

"I'm a man of science. And my reasoning tells me that I haven't the slightest idea," he replied. "I will need to conduct proper research to get to the heart of the matter."

He glanced at his watch.

"It is also well past my noon engagement. I'll leave my assistant to proceed with the initial investigation and file it at the bureau. Do have a good day."

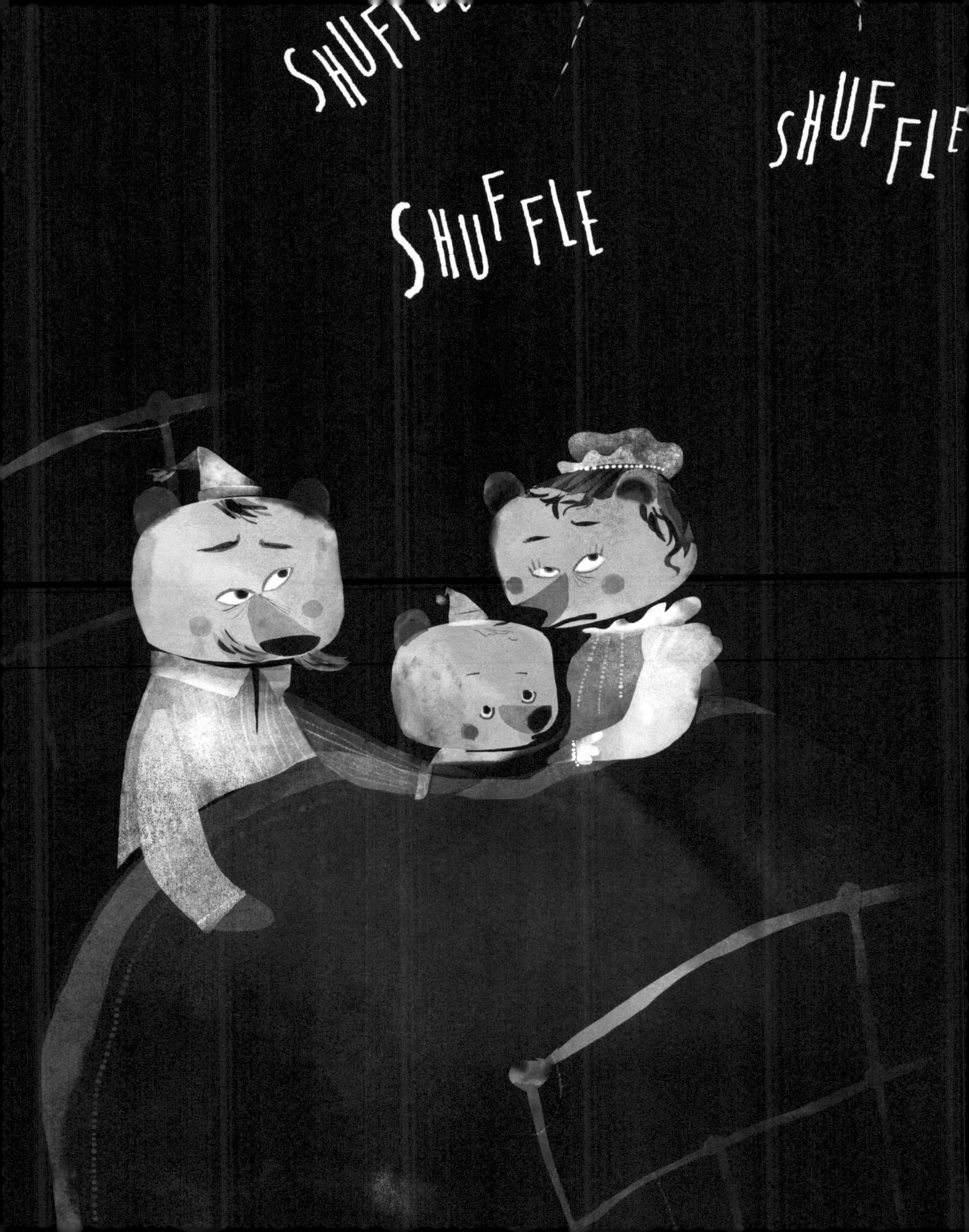
SHUFFLE
SHUFFLE

That night the Bears all slept in one room. And Papa Bear was nearly asleep when something in the attic jolted him awake.

He heard shuffling noises.

Papa Bear shook Mama Bear awake. "It's upstairs."

Baby Bear woke up as well and heard the shuffling continue.

"If there's something that you want from us, tell us!" Papa Bear yelled at the ceiling.

There was now silence.

"Just leave us alone," Mama Bear pleaded. "Please!"

Suddenly the dresser began to rattle.

"What do you want from us?!"

The dresser shook more violently, spilling out the drawers and all its contents.

"Stop!" Baby Bear screamed.

The dresser erupted into an epileptic frenzy and then collapsed with a swift violence.

When the crash settled, Papa Bear could see tiny hand prints all over the wall scored with scratches.

Papa Bear tried gentle reasoning.

"Please. Tell us, what do you want from us?"

RUMBLE

RUMBLE

RUMBLE

But there was only a reply of scratching noises from where the hand prints were.

It sounded as though a small creature was trapped in a wall.

Skritch... *Skritch*... *Skritch*....

With rage, Papa Bear grabbed a golf iron and attacked the wall. He kept striking the wall until a hole became visible. Then he abruptly stopped.

There was something nestled in the wall.

Old dusty envelopes.

Somehow they had fallen into the cracks of the wall.

All the envelopes showed the written address:

328 PORRIDGE LANE.

"328... 3.. 28..." Papa Bear mumbled with recognition. "Porridge. Porridge Lane... "

Papa Bear began reading the contents of the letter.

Dear Sister,

My hope of ever seeing you and Mama and Papa again is starting to fade. All I carry in my dying heart are memories of us. Do you remember the time we all slept together in Mama and Papa's bed and made up stories until we fell asleep? Do you recall that? I am especially fond of the time when we both sat in the same chair reading together until the old chair broke under us.

I don't know how long they'll keep me here. They keep telling me they will let me go soon, though I doubt soon will ever come. Has anyone searched for me?

I miss you terribly.

From the envelope, Papa Bear also pulled out a locket.

Mama Bear opened it and pulled out a long wisp of blonde hair. She choked back her tears.

"Poor girl…"

"What happened to her, Mama?" Baby Bear asked.

BOOM! BOOM! BOOM! A loud knock suddenly startled everyone.

It was the Inspector. He had returned with news clippings, one which showed the headline,

"THE GOLDILOCKS KIDNAP."

He soon began to relay the story that long ago, a wealthy eccentric couple who resided in this very estate wanted a child desperately but couldn't.

The day they saw the twins and their golden hair, they decided to kidnap one of them and kept her as their very own.

They kept the little girl in the cellar, and she died of sickness under captivity. Fearing the consequences, they secretly buried her in the garden patch until the authorities finally apprehended them.

GOLDILOCKS
BODY FOUND

M. M
S HOR

JN COMMUNI

JO

KIDNAPF

UNSOLVED

CHARGE

GOLDILOCK CASE

"You mean they buried her in the garden patch like the one outside?" Papa Bear asked.

The Inspector nodded.

"We were not able to find the real parents. They were believed to be immigrants from the Old World; it is believed that they went into seclusion, so stricken they were with grief and loss."

"And they never knew about the kid-nappers and the death of their daughter?" Mama Bear asked.

The Inspector removed his hat.

"From what we gathered, the other twin sister is alive, living with the parents," he replied. "But as to their whereabouts, we haven't the slightest clue."

Papa Bear glanced at the address on the envelope.

"328..." he said to himself.

Though it took some time, the 328 Porridge Lane address and the clues in the letters helped Papa Bear and the Inspector eventually locate Goldilocks' family in the Old World.

The family expressed deep gratitude for the letters and for the locket. They told Papa Bear that the letters had truly lifted their sorrows. They felt as though their daughter had indeed returned home at last.

Papa Bear had felt that too.

That night, the Bears slept soundly, recalling now with fondness that some time ago, someone came into their house.

Ate their porridge.

Sat in their chairs.

Slept in their beds.

And that someone was a little girl longing to be home.